118
25.64

S0-BOC-665

Roselle Public Library District
40 S. Park Street
Roselle, IL 60172

Ruby Tuesday
Readers

Monster Molly's BIG Day Out

By Dee Reid

Reading Consultant: Beth Walker Gambro

Ruby Tuesday Books

Published in 2018 by Ruby Tuesday Books Ltd.

Copyright © 2018 Ruby Tuesday Books Ltd.

All rights reserved. No part of this publication may be reproduced in whole or in part, stored in any retrieval system, or transmitted in any form or by any means, electronic, mechanical, photocopying, recording, or otherwise, without written permission from the publisher.

Design and illustrations: Emma Randall
Editor: Ruth Owen
Production: John Lingham

Library of Congress Control Number: 2018946147
Print (hardback) ISBN 978-1-78856-054-2
Print (paperback) ISBN 978-1-78856-071-9
eBook ISBN 978-1-78856-055-9

Printed and published in the United States of America.

For further information including rights and permissions requests, please contact our Customer Services Department at 877-337-8577.

Molly was sad.

Let's go to
the park.

6

I am happy!

Molly sat in the bus.

Max sat on the bus.

q

Max walked to the park.

Molly ran to the park.

Molly went on the little swing.

Max went on the big swing.

17

Max went in a big puddle.

Can you find the opposites?

happy

hot

wet

little

up

big

cold

dry

sad

down

Can you remember?

Who was sad?

How did Molly and Max get to the park?

Who sat on the bus?

Who went on the big swing?

Why did Molly laugh at Max?

Can you read these words?

big	is	on
the	was	went